Happy 5th Birthday
Elise
Love you Always!
Nana and Popeye

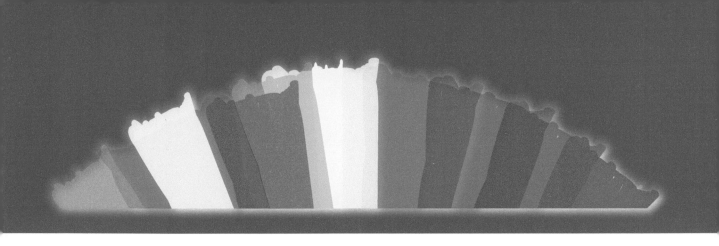

GEROME'S RAINBOW ™

STORY BY STEPHANIE LOGSDON

PICTURES & ILLUSTRATIONS BY M. E. B. STOTTMANN

Published by

"Gerome's Rainbow"

For information:
Baxter's Corner,
P.O. Box 223,
Harrods Creek, KY 40027
www.BaxtersCorner.com

Library of Congress Control Number: 2019910915

ISBN 978-1-938647-30-7

March 2020

Dedicated to my two boys who have enabled me to see the unique colors of the rainbow in each and every person.

"Time for art class,"
    said Mr. McBoom.
The students' cheers echoed
    across the classroom.

To the carpet they scurried
    and sat one by one,
then looked at their teacher
    prepared to have fun.

"This project is special,"
    said McBoom with a grin.
"First, let me explain,
    and then we'll begin."

"Your job is to make
    a picture of you.
We all are a mixture,
    of red, yellow, and blue.

"These primary colors
    can make many hues.
Blend one with another
    and watch how they fuse."

"Now look in the mirror,
    then pick out your shade.
And remember to always
    accept how you're made."

Looking quite puzzled
    their eyes focused down.
There was paper all over -
    pink, blue, red, and brown.

Ally grabbed green.
　　Fred reached for it, too.
But then someone whispered,
　　"That color is Ewwwww!"

Both looked to the left.
　　"Now that was quite rude!"
But there was no "sorry."
　　They continued to feud.

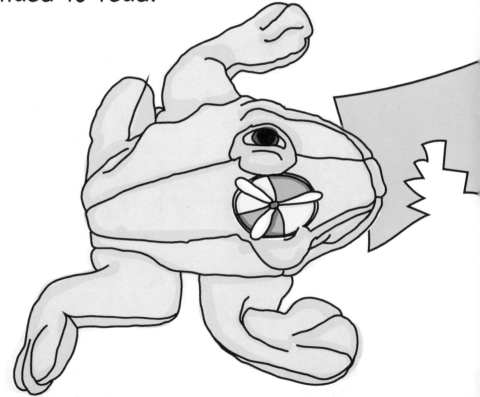

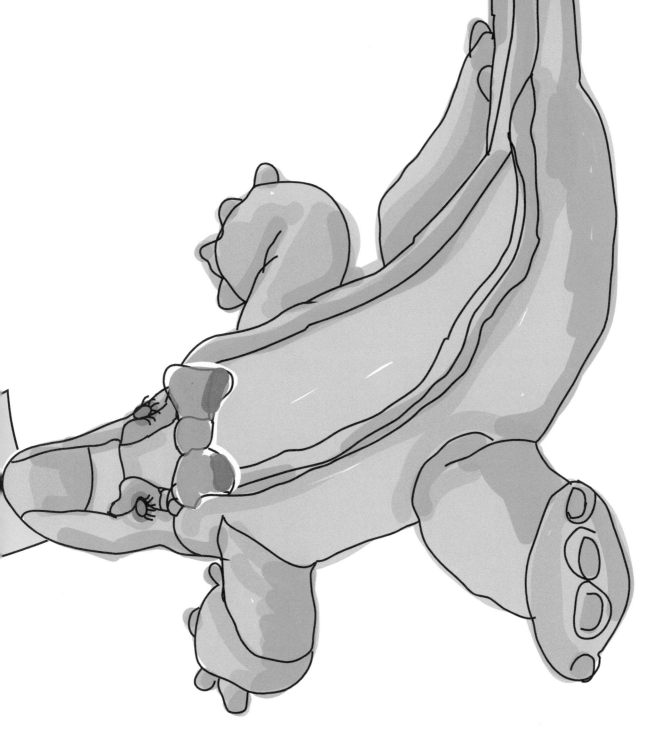

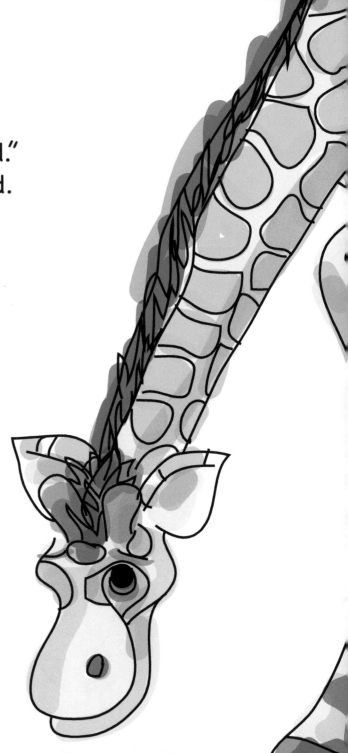

"Who would pick brown?"
Another kid said,
"Brown looks like the mud."
Gerome hung his head.

"At least we're not gray,"
    said Tajo to Gerome.
Ellema overheard
    and wished she were home.

It didn't stop there.
    The arguments grew.
Some poked fun at pink.
    Others belittled blue.

Gerome used his loud voice,
    "Let's all get a grip!"
But it was too late.
    Paper started to rip.

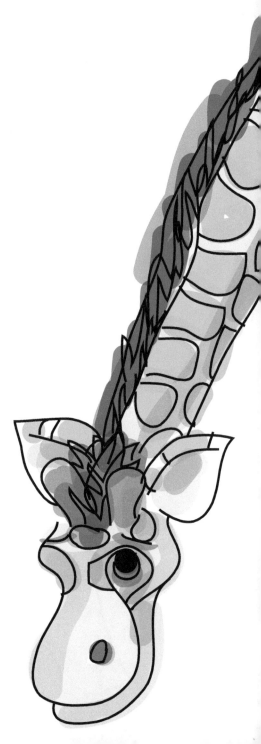

It swished through the air
    like embers at night.
Paper swirled to the ground.
    What a horrible sight!

The colors lay broken;
    spread from wall to the door.
No longer whole paper,
    shreds covered the floor!

They swept all the paper,
    but it was too late.
The pile was too big
    to hide from their fate.

19

McBoom shook his head,
    then glanced at the ground.
He stared at his students,
    who all looked straight down.

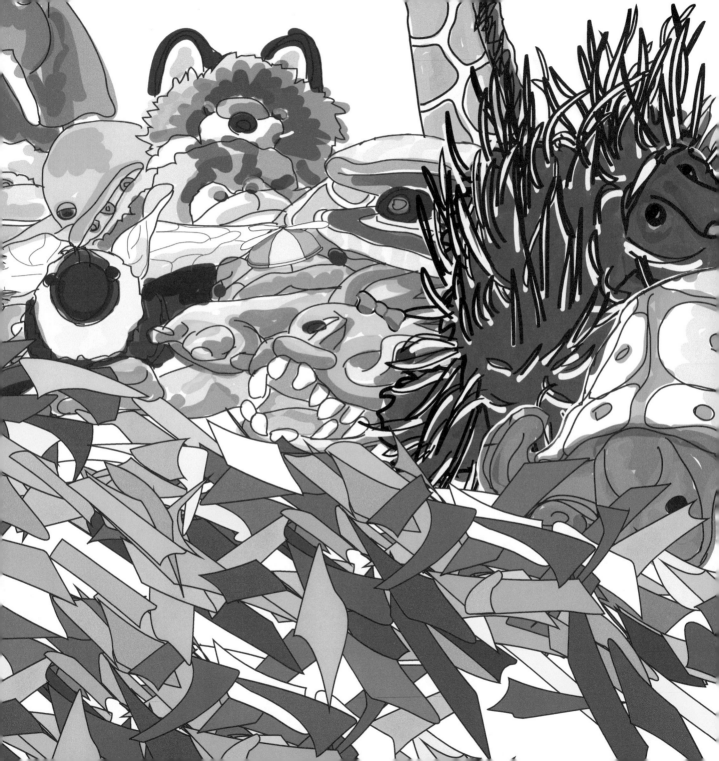

Ellema sneezed softly.
    Ally's tail twitched side-to-side.
It seemed very clear
    each wanted to hide.

Without a word spoken
    they lined up at the door.
Some stepped on the paper
    as they all crossed the floor.

The school day was done,
    and everyone was sad.
Each slowly slunk home.
    They all felt very bad.

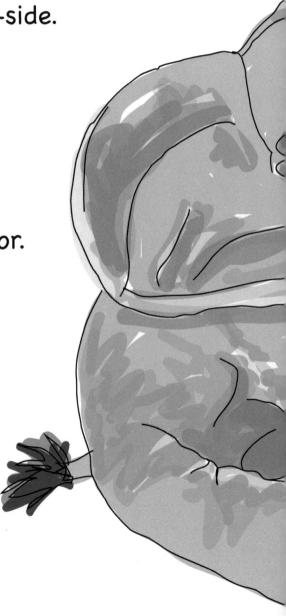

That night Gerome wept.
    He thought of the day.
He had watched his friends fight,
    and it wasn't okay.

The sun was bright yellow.
    The grass shades of green.
But without light to reflect them,
    colors could not be seen.

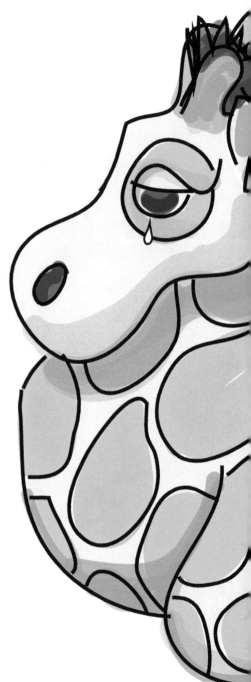

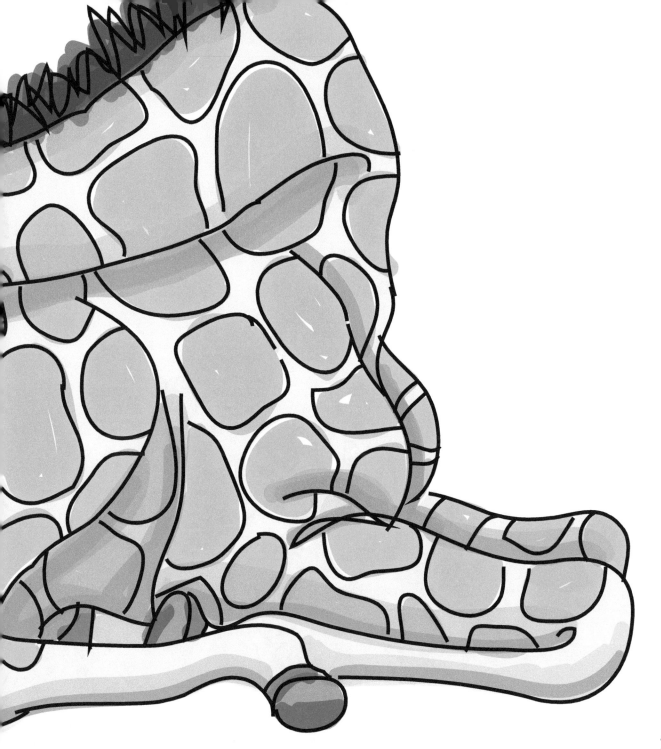

Gerome tried to imagine
    if everyone looked the same.
It would be quite awful.
    His heart filled with shame.

Gerome knew that each color
    was truly meant to be.
No matter the outside,
    he knew acceptance was key.

He had an idea,
   that was thoughtful and kind.
He raced to school early.
   He knew just who to find.

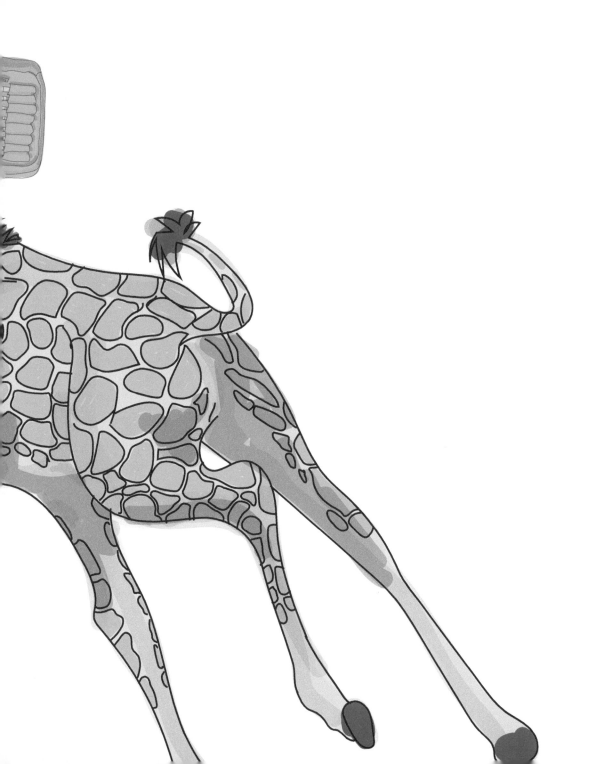

When he saw Ellema
    He whispered his plan.
She smiled at him kindly,
    and then they began.

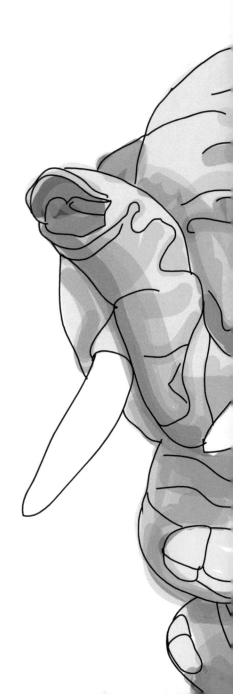

They snuck into class
   without much time at all.
They had to move fast
   to make morning roll call.

Grabbing scissors and glue
   Gerome cut and they pasted.
He thought as he snipped
   no color would be wasted.

Then Ellema used her trunk
    to suck in all the pieces.
And in true Ellema style
    she blew out six sneezes.

Some paper flew high.
    Some paper blew low.
And each tiny shred landed
    exactly where it should go.

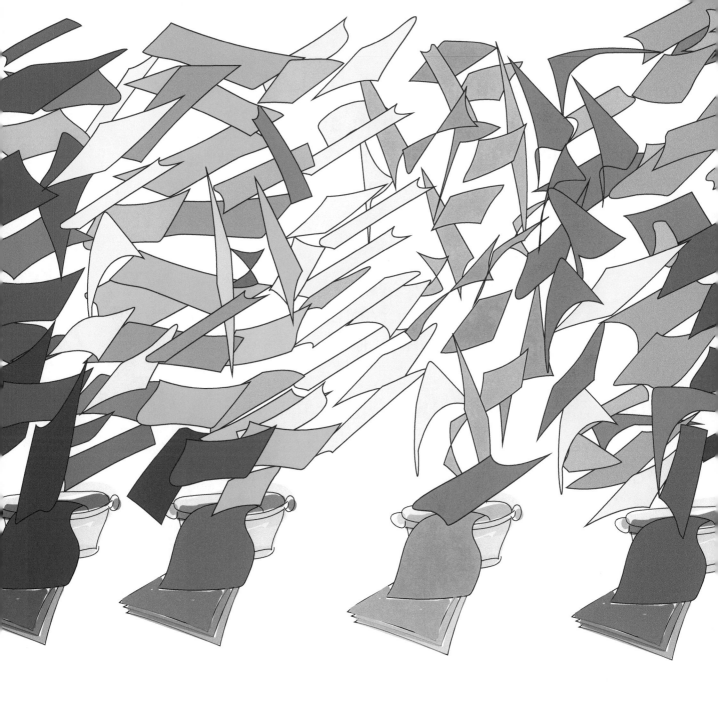

35

When the students arrived
　　they looked 'round in awe
and smiled with amazement
　　at the splendor they saw.

Then each student clapped
　　because everyone knew
when Gerome saw a problem,
　　he knew just what to do.

Gerome knew all the colors
　　were part of the whole,
and a world without colors
　　wouldn't have any soul.

The students all decided
    it was best to forgive.
Because being closed-minded
    was no way to live.

They all learned a lesson,
    and not just about pride.
They learned to accept others
    no matter the color outside.

Everyone on Earth
    is a mix of red, yellow, and blue,
a blend of primary colors.
    Gerome knew this to be true.

Just then through the window
    the students felt a warm glow,
and the sunlight revealed
    Gerome's beautiful RAINBOW!

Each **Baxter's Corner** book includes a special *GoBeyond* section to intentionally spur conversation between an adult and child. You and your child will experience many magical moments together as you share thoughts and ideas about the story you just read together.

GO BEYOND...

TRANSFORM STORYTIME

43

Fun facts about rainbows

- Rainbows form when light reflects, or bounces off, water droplets. That's why you often see rainbows after it has rained, and around waterfalls that spray water droplets into the air.

- No two people see a rainbow in exactly the same way.

- Rainbows look like arches when viewed from the ground, but they are actually circles.

- A rainbow is not an object that can be touched.

- There are at least twelve types of rainbows. Some examples include red rainbows, fogbows, and twinned rainbows.

What do you think?

Search for specific examples from the story to answer questions 1-3. Use questions 4-7 to discuss the importance of acceptance and what it means to accept others.

1. What did Mr. McBoom want his students to create?
2. How did Ellema feel when Tajo said, "at least we're not gray"?
3. What did Gerome and Ellema create with the scraps of paper?

For discussion

4. Have you ever seen someone be teased before?
5. If so, how did they feel?
6. Why do you think Gerome created a rainbow?
7. How can you help others feel accepted?

Find referral pages for answers on next page.

Answers for "What do you think?"

Use text and illustrations on the following pages to help answer the questions.

1. What did Mr. McBoom want his students to create?	Page 10
2. How did Ellema feel when Tajo said, "at least we're not gray"?	Page 16
3. What did Gerome and Ellema create with the scraps of paper?	Page 34

Discussion Questions

Use **Stop & Think** on page 59 to discuss acceptance of others. Gerome understood that it was important to accept others just the way they are. He encouraged his friends to accept and celebrate their differences.

Acceptance

Could you imagine a world with only one flavor of ice cream? What a scary thought!

Luckily, there are over 1,000 flavors of ice cream in the world. While some people love strawberry ice cream, others love mint chocolate chip. If you think about it, people are a lot like ice cream. Ice cream flavors may be different, but in the end, they are all ice cream. Accepting everyone, even those who are different from you might be hard to do sometimes, but in the end everyone is human and deserves respect and acceptance.

What is your favorite flavor ice cream?

What is your best friends favorite flavor?

Are they the same flavor, or are they different?

If they are different, is that okay?

What is something about you that is unique?

What is something unique about your friend?

Draw a picture or write a nice note to your friend telling them how special they are to you.

We are all just like ice cream

What does acceptance look like?

Just like all of the characters in *Gerome's Rainbow* are different, people are different, too. We are different shapes, colors, backgrounds, and religions. Acceptance looks like everyone getting along and respecting each other, even though we are not the same.

When we are having trouble practicing acceptance we:
- think before we speak.
- treat others with kindness, even if we are nervous because someone looks or acts different than we do.

Can you understand
how others might think differently than you?

Could you have a good friend that looks or thinks
differently than you?

Can you imagine what it might be like
to be judged because you are different?

Understanding how others feel is called empathy. People can show empathy by listening and trying to see the world as someone else sees it. Empathy helps people accept others.

Where in the story does Gerome show empathy?

(Hint- check out page 24)

Rainbow Craft

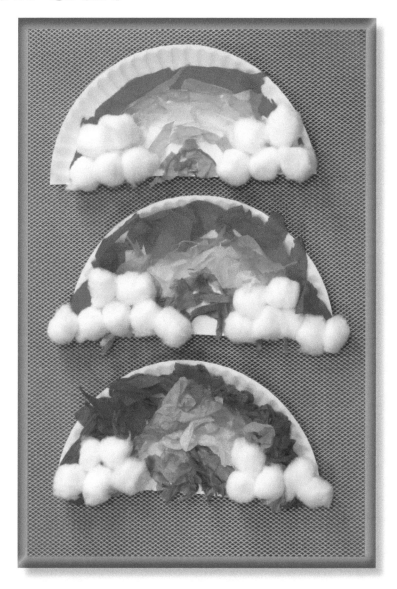

Rainbow Craft continued

Materials

Scissors

Glue

Paper plates

Crayons or markers

Tissue paper (multiple colors; ripped into pieces)

Cotton balls

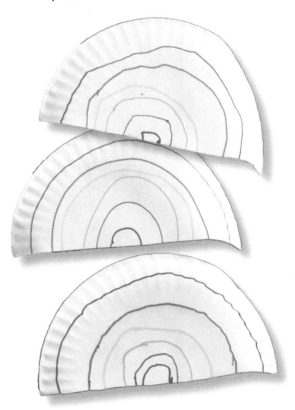

Rainbow Craft continued

Directions

1. Arrange the crayons or markers in the order of a rainbow - red, orange, yellow, green, blue, and purple.

2. Starting with the last color, purple, draw a small circle (about the size of a half dollar) in the middle of the paper plate.

3. Next, using the blue, draw a new circle around the purple circle, about 1 inch apart.

4. Do the same with green, yellow, orange, and red until there are six circles going from the inside to the outside of the paper plate.

5. Cut the plate in half. You now have two rainbow templates to guide you.

6. Glue pieces of corresponding colored tissue paper to each line.

7. Glue 6-10 cotton balls on the bottoms of each side to look like clouds.

When you are finished get pictures of your friends to attach underneath the rainbow.

Adults - help younger children according to their skills.

How we see things

For this activity, you will need a pair of sunglasses. Put on the sunglasses and look around you. How do the objects in the room appear?

Most likely, the objects in the room appear darker, or are more difficult to see when you are wearing the sunglasses. When you take off the glasses, the objects appear to be brighter, and it is easier to see details that you might have missed while wearing the sunglasses.

Sunglasses affect the way we see things. Just like sunglasses, any thoughts or ideas we hold can affect what we see and think about situations and people.

Consider these situations:

- You go to a new school and are told by a friend that a certain teacher is mean or boring. How might that affect what you think when you meet that teacher for the first time?

- You see someone in a wheelchair. Would you change what you think if you learned that person is an award-winning athlete?

- You meet a new classmate who is wearing old or dirty clothes. If you learned that person had lost all their clothing in a recent fire at their house, would that change what you think?

These are examples of how we can miss important information about someone when we first meet them. So, before you form an opinion about a new person or unfamiliar situation, be sure to "take off your sunglasses!"

Note to adult: Help the younger children with the sunglasses as they may harm the eyes.

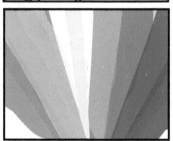

ACCEPTANCE - There are many
wonderful ways that each person is different. Acceptance means we welcome, include and do not make fun of someone just because they look, think or act differently than we are used to. When we look beyond what is different, we usually find there are many ways we are alike.

STOP & THINK – You always have a choice about
how to treat someone who may look, think or act differently than you.

- Do you know other families that are different than yours?

- Where would we get new ideas for stories, games, or new foods to try if everyone was the same?

- How would you feel if you were the one who was different from everyone else and they made fun of you or did not include you?

Here are some choices you have when you meet someone who is different from you.

- Say hello and introduce yourself.

- Tell them about your favorite things and ask the other person about what they like.

- If you notice someone sitting alone or being left out, invite them to join in.

- It is okay to ask about what is different to help you better understand someone.

What other choices do you have?

a Baxter story

What A Tree It Will Be!
The thin bundle of branches isn't exactly what the kids wanted. Mr. McBoom encourages each student to add their own special touch. Together they create the perfect tree.

Cooperation

Oakley in Knots
– It's polite to shake hands, but which hand should an eight-handed octopus use? Oakley the octopus worries himself into a knot as he considers his options. His classmates laugh at his predicament.

Respect

Ally Alone
Ally the alligator does not have a dad to invite to school, he is feels very alone. Everything turns around when Ally chooses to focus on what she has instead of what she is missing.

Resilience

Ellema Sneezes
Ellema the elephant suffers from allergies. When she sneezes, everything around her blows away. Once she learns to control her sneezes, everything calms until Kite Day when she saves the day.

Respect

Sideways Fred
Fred the frog can't wait to jump just like the older frogs. But one of Fred's new legs is shorter than the other. Instead of giving up, when told he will never be able to jump straight, he figures out a special way to jump.

Determination

Gerome Sticks His Neck Out
Gerome does not like the attention he draws due to his height. He finds a way to keep a low profile but knows he isn't being genuine. He is finally able to fully embrace his height, when his concern for another becomes greater than his concern for himself.

Compassion

What people are saying about Baxter's Corner books

"Excellent, sweet stories to get discussions going."

Barbara Freas

"Clever ways to teach important lessons."

Susan Catucci

"Thought-provoking without preachiness."

Elizabeth

"Wow, interesting concept!"

Lisa Hascall

"What a clever way to teach children."

Debra Daugherty

"I should have read these as a child. Great way to teach little minds."

Julianne Noel

"These stories are designed to teach great lessons."

Laura Ostrem

"This seems like a good way to catch the attention of kids who might not be receptive to a typical messenger."

Jamie Kiffel-Alcheh

CPSIA information can be obtained
at www.ICGtesting.com
Printed in the USA
LVHW072056090420
652870LV00002B/2